They're So Flamboyant

By **Michael Genhart, PhD**

Illustrated by **Tony Neal**

Magination Press – Washington, DC – American Psychological Association

To being flamboyant. Be pretty.
Be pink. Be proud!!—*MG*

For Olive—*TN*

Books for Kids From the
American Psychological Association

maginationpress.org

Magination Press is a registered trademark of the American Psychological Association. Order books at maginationpress.org, or call 1-800-374-2721.
Book design by Rachel Ross
Printed by Sonic Media Solutions, Inc., Medford, NY

Library of Congress Cataloging-in-Publication Data
Names: Genhart, Michael, author. | Neal, Tony, illustrator.
Title: They're so flamboyant / by Michael Genhart ; illustrations by Tony Neal.
Other titles: They are so flamboyant
Description: [Washington, D.C.]: Magination Press, an imprint of the American Psychological Association, 2021. | Summary: Follows the reaction of a neighborhood of birds, from a congress of crows to a gaggle of geese, when a flamboyance of flamingos moves in.
Identifiers: LCCN 2021007020 (print) | LCCN 2021007021 (ebook) | ISBN 9781433832789 (hardcover) | ISBN 9781433837586 (ebook)
Subjects: CYAC: Toleration—Fiction. | Birds—Fiction. | Animals—Nomenclature—Fiction. | English language—Collective nouns—Fiction. | Neighborhoods—Fiction.
Classification: LCC PZ7.1.G47 Th 2021 (print) | LCC PZ7.1.G47 (ebook) | DDC [E]—dc23
LC record available at https://lccn.loc.gov/2021007020
LC ebook record available at https://lccn.loc.gov/2021007021

Manufactured in the United States of America
10 9 8 7 6 5 4 3 2 1

flam•boy•ant – (of a person—or bird!—
or their behavior) tending to attract attention because of
their confidence, exuberance, and stylishness

When a flamboyance of flamingos
flew into the neighborhood...

And a dole of doves discussed their dissent.

Our peace has been totally disrupted!

All the commotion
caused a pandemonium
of parrots.

They are
so pink!

The charm of finches
was not at all charmed.

Their necks are
so long!

And the brood of chickens clucked and sighed.

Always preening, preening, preening!

A scream of swifts shrieked!

Enough with all this flamboyance!

And the unkindness of ravens
was just kind of unkind.

Gawk! Stay in your own
neighborhood! Gawk!

The neighbors were so ruffled by the newcomers that a squadron of pelicans patrolled by day.

First moving trucks, and now food trucks?

And by night, a watch of nightingales stayed alert.

Don't flamingos ever sleep?

Finally, the band of
jays decided it was
time for the neighbors
to flock together.

With tails unfurled, the pride
of peacocks took the lead.

A waddle of penguins brought up the rear
as a venue of vultures ventured over.

If only we had legs like
those flamingos!

The mob of emus was ready for a fight.

We can take them— easy!

The gulp of cormorants gulped and then dove, ducking the dispute.

Uh oh, here we go!

Suddenly the front door
swung open wide.

But before any skirmish could start, the chime of wrens chimed,

Stay calm.

Thankfully, the wisdom of owls had the smarts to bring a heaping plate of algae for the new neighbors.

Then the friendly flamboyance
of flamingos exclaimed,

Who Knew? A Sampling of Bird Groupings

It turns out, a group of birds is more than a "flock." Birders have all kinds of names for groupings of birds—names that capture their behavior and personalities. Sometimes the different group names have to do with whether birds are in flight, resting in a tree, or if they are on land or at sea.

What other bird group names do you know?

Birds of prey (like hawks, falcons) — cast, cauldron, kettle

Buzzards — wake

Chickens — peep, brood, clutch

Cormorants — flight, gulp, sunning, swim

Cranes — herd, dance, sedge

Crows — murder, congress, horde, muster, cauldron

Doves — bevy, cote, flight, dole, piteousness

Ducks — raft, team, paddling (on the water), badling, brace

Eagles — convocation, congregation, aerie

Emus — mob

Finches — charm, trembling

Flamingos — flamboyance, stand, pat

Geese — skein (in flight), wedge, gaggle (on the ground), plump (flying close together)

Gulls — colony, squabble, flotilla, scavenging, gullery

Herons — siege, sedge, scattering

Jays — band, party, scold, cast

Larks — bevy, exaltation, ascension, happiness

Loons — asylum, cry, water dance

Nightingales — watch

Owls — parliament, wisdom, study, bazaar, glaring, stare

Parrots — pandemonium, company, prattle

Peacocks — muster, ostentation, pride, party

Pelicans — squadron, pod, scoop

Penguins — colony, huddle, creche, waddle, rookery (on land), raft (at sea)

Quails — battery, drift, flush, rout, shake, bevy, covey

Ravens — murder, congress, horde, unkindness

Sparrows — host, quarrel, knot, flutter, crew, tribe

Storks — mustering, phalanx (migrating)

Swallows — flight, gulp

Swans — wedge, ballet, lamentation, whiteness, regatta

Swifts — flock, scream

Turkeys — rafter, gobble, gang, posse

Vultures — wake, venue (resting in a tree), kettle (in flight), committee

Woodpeckers — descent, drumming

Wrens — herd, chime

Note to Readers & Birders (!)

They're So Flamboyant is a story about inclusion, exclusion, and the stereotypes, fears, and assumptions that can lead to discrimination. The new neighbors are flamboyant flamingos who are simply being their self-confident, awesome selves. The other bird groups are quick to form first impressions about the flamingos and miss out on seeing who their new neighbors really are: warm, friendly, and welcoming. When the birds have a chance to spend more time with the flamingos at their party, their fears dissolve and their attitudes become much more positive.

Indirectly, They're So Flamboyant also refers to being "flamboyant"— a word traditionally used in a derogatory sense to describe someone who is gay. This story playfully reclaims the word and shows the flamboyant flamingos as gracious and neighborly, modeling positive and welcoming behavior for the other birds. It should be noted, however, that it is not the responsibility of those being discriminated against to make the others comfortable. The flamingos don't change who they are and shouldn't have to; instead, it is the other birds who change by spending time with and learning about their new neighbors.

Conversations with children about the assumptions and stereotypes that can lead to excluding behavior are vitally important if we are to live in a world that is more inclusive, fair, and welcoming. These conversations about differences and diversity should be straightforward, open, and honest. Whether one is talking about age, race, ethnicity, sexual orientation, body type, disability, income level, or religion, adults can have age-appropriate chats with children in a natural way, as they notice the world around them and ask questions. Since stress associated with discrimination can profoundly affect self-esteem, talking with children about diversity as well as modeling inclusivity can help kids learn to appreciate people from all backgrounds.

Michael Genhart, PhD, is a licensed clinical psychologist in private practice in San Francisco. He is the acclaimed author of many picture books, including *Love is Love, I See You, Ouch! Moments, So Many Smarts!, Cake & I Scream!, Accordionly,* and *Rainbow,* among other titles. He lives with his flamboyant family in Marin County, California. Visit michaelgenhart.com, @MJGenhart on Facebook, @MGenhart on Twitter, and @MichaelGenhart on Instagram.

Tony Neal is a graphic artist and illustrator. He loves to create charming characters in whimsical scenes and tell stories with his pictures. He lives in South Leicestershire, England. Visit tonyneal.co.uk, and @TonyNealArt on Facebook, Twitter, and Instagram.

Magination Press is the children's book imprint of the American Psychological Association. APA works to advance psychology as a science and profession and as a means of promoting health and human welfare. Magination Press books reach young readers and their parents and caregivers to make navigating life's challenges a little easier. It's the combined power of psychology and literature that makes a Magination Press book special. Visit maginationpress.org and @MaginationPress on Facebook, Twitter, Instagram, and Pinterest.